IN THE BAR OF A TOKYO HOTEL

BY TENNESSEE WILLIAMS

DPS
DRAMATISTS PLAY SERVICE

ISBN 978-0-8222-0562-3
www.dramatists.com
www.concordtheatricals.com

Please refer to the back of this volume for further information.

IN THE BAR OF A TOKYO HOTEL was first presented by Richard Lee Marks and Henry Jaffe at the Eastside Playhouse, in New York City, on May 11, 1969. It was directed by Herbert Machiz; sets and lighting were by Neil Peter Jampolis; the costumes were by Stanley Simmons; and the musical effects by Hayward Morris. The cast, in order of appearance, was as follows:

BAR-MAN .... Jon Lee
MIRIAM .... Anne Meacham
MARK .... Donald Madden
HAWAIIAN LADY .... Elsa Raven
LEONARD .... Lester Rawlins

TIME: Spring
PLACE: Tokyo

PART ONE
Midday

PART TWO
Noon—A Few Days Later

IN THE BAR OF A TOKYO HOTEL

PART I

A smartly and exotically dressed American woman is seated at a small round table in a small area of intense light. She is glossily handsome. She wears a hat crowned with blue-black cock feathers. The Bar-man, behind a bar of polished bamboo, is in a pin-spot of light. He is young and his appearance suggests an Oriental idol. He raises a metal shaker, a few moments after the rise of the curtain, as if to signal the start of the scene.

MIRIAM. I like this room.

BAR-MAN. Thank you.

MIRIAM. There is an atmosphere of such vitality in Tokyo.

BAR-MAN. Thank you.

MIRIAM. You understand and speak English remarkably well.

BAR-MAN. Thank you.

MIRIAM. You have a very impressive suicide rate.

BAR-MAN. Thank you.

MIRIAM. I don't think you understood what I said.

BAR-MAN. I was.

MIRIAM. I said that you have a very impressive rate of suicide in—

BAR-MAN. In America there is no suicide rate?

MIRIAM. In America what we have is an explosion of vitality which is world wide.

BAR-MAN. Many cowboys exported?

MIRIAM. Ha-ha, yes, it could be put that way. "Many cowboys exported!" Yes, but speaking for myself, I don't really need an atmosphere of vitality around me.

BAR-MAN. You have enough in yourself?

MIRIAM. Let's say that I have enough and a little more than enough.

BAR-MAN. —I am not astonished.

MIRIAM. Hmmm. How many hours of sleep do you need a night?

BAR-MAN. Thank you for being interested, but why are you interested?

MIRIAM. I'm always interested. For me, only four hours of sleep are necessary.

BAR-MAN. You waken in the dark?

MIRIAM. Not usually. You see, I go to bed late.

BAR-MAN. You make excursions at night?

MIRIAM. Yes, I'm restless at night. What's your name?

BAR-MAN. I am the Bar-man.

MIRIAM. Yes, I've noticed you are. Why don't you look for an occupation that's not so confining?

BAR-MAN. Thank you.

MIRIAM. You're welcome. See what I'm doing? I'm taking out of my handbag a mirror. *(She removes a large mirror from her bag.)*

BAR-MAN. Why are you staring at me?

MIRIAM. I like to see what is going on about me in the circle of light.

BAR-MAN. Excuse me while I. *(He carries a tray of drinks off* R.*)*

MIRIAM. Yes. The best idea. Cable to Leonard. Place in his hands. *(The Bar-man returns with the tray. She observes him in the mirror.)* Hmmm. Your activity with the shaker is very distracting.

BAR-MAN. Pardon me. I am the Bar-man.

MIRIAM. "Inner resources of serenity." Some professor mentioned them to me once. Hog-wash, wash a hog in it, don't turn it on me. "Inner resources of serenity" is a polite way of describing a lack of vital energy. There may be exceptions but.

BAR-MAN. The light from the mirror is in my eyes.

MIRIAM. For light in your eyes be grateful. I am happy to lower the focus of the. Don't stand behind the bar.

BAR-MAN. My instruction is.

MIRIAM. Your employer wouldn't object if you stood in front of the bar. *(After a moment, the Bar-man moves in front of the bar.)*

BAR-MAN. —The light from the mirror burns through my clothes.

MIRIAM. Are you sure it isn't my observation of you?

BAR-MAN. I am.

MIRIAM. You are. So am I. Will you please bring me some ice for my drink?

BAR-MAN. With pleasure and precaution and a little delay. *(He has started into the wings with a tray of cocktails. Miriam takes a small pipe from her handbag and fills it from a pouch.)*

MIRIAM. Hmmm.

BAR-MAN. There is a party of diplomats in the restaurant, excuse me please.

MIRIAM. I will excuse you if you don't stay long. *(He exits with drinks.)* Hmm. Difficult, yes, but unobtainable, no— A little Panama Red. *(After she has taken a few puffs of the little pipe, the Bar-man returns.)* Hmmm. Diplomats. Young?

BAR-MAN. Venerable.

MIRIAM. I haven't heard that word in a long long time.

BAR-MAN. Perhaps there are a number of words in English, not idiomatic, that it would not be useless for you to.

MIRIAM. I like the idioms of my native country.

BAR-MAN. You are smoking a pipe of marijuana.

MIRIAM. A pipe of Panama Red.

BAR-MAN. The pleasure of a guest is usually my pleasure, but will you do for me the kindness?

MIRIAM. I will put it out for you. Put it out means extinguish.

BAR-MAN. Thank you.

MIRIAM. Panama Red is not essential to my.

BAR-MAN. Vitality. Natural to your nature.

MIRIAM. Hmmmm. No. I don't say it doesn't augment it, but it.

BAR-MAN. Thank you.

MIRIAM. I will teach you the idioms of English. Some of them centuries old. Venerable. The important idioms can be learned very.

BAR-MAN. Not necessary, but thank you.

MIRIAM. Are you married?

BAR-MAN. I am engaged. And faithful.

MIRIAM. A terrible mistake. For marriage, some preliminary instruction is necessary.

BAR-MAN. Thank you. I have had the necessary instruction.

MIRIAM. There are fairly good instructors and there are brilliant instructors.

BAR-MAN. It is kind of you to be interested in my instruction. *(He exits with another tray of drinks. From time to time a wind sweeps through the bar. Ornamented glass pendants—suspended from the arch of a door leading offstage—chatter musically when the wind blows through. This is used as a way of underlining or punctuating. Each time the pendants sound, Miriam touches the feathers on her hat and makes her humming sound: then rearranges the bracelets on her arms and moves her head from side to side more noticeably. Now the Bar-man returns.)*

MIRIAM. I have noticed a lot of very stout women in the hotel, their doors open on the corridors. They sit on the edge of their beds, doing nothing at all.

BAR-MAN. Ladies from Hawaii.

MIRIAM. Just sitting. No energy in them to get up and be on the go?

BAR-MAN. The ladies are a party of.

MIRIAM. Not enough vitality for an argument, or even a conversation.

BAR-MAN. Nice ladies from Hawaii.

MIRIAM. I didn't say they weren't nice. Being nice or not nice is. What I said about the Hawaiian ladies is that they should be up and about. They should be on the move. Did their husbands suggest this trip to Japan to them?

BAR-MAN. I think their husbands are satisfied with the.

MIRIAM. Perhaps in Hawaii a very fat wife is what we call, in America, a status symbol. *(Hawaiian Lady enters D. R. She wears a dress printed with large flowers.)*

BAR-MAN. That is nothing I know. *(Hawaiian Lady crosses to arch, exits.)*

MIRIAM. My god, one of them off her bed, it must have collapsed so she had to get on the move. Probably has no idea of where she's headed. Where I'm headed is something I always know.

BAR-MAN. Japan has other places.

MIRIAM. I've been told that I shouldn't miss Kyoto. The person, the acquaintance, the man that mentioned Kyoto to me said that Kyoto is a place of lovely old pagodas and flowering trees in flower at this time of.

BAR-MAN. Yes, go to Kyoto.

MIRIAM. Yes, I'll go to Kyoto on an evening train. I love the clackety-clack of the wheels and the cool wind through the windows. I hope there's a train leaving at.

BAR-MAN. The concierge can give you the schedules.

MIRIAM. The concierge is venerable as the diplomats.

BAR-MAN. The concierge will be happy to give you the.

MIRIAM. I'll go this evening.

BAR-MAN. It is possible to go more early.

MIRIAM. I prefer an evening train. Kyoto. To absorb Kyoto wouldn't take me long. A woman of my vitality absorbs a place quickly. I could absorb a pagoda in a minute. Well, if I walked around it, a few minutes more. That sounds as if I meant superficial absorption, but.

BAR-MAN. Some of the pagodas are five or six hundred years old.

MIRIAM. Venerable, but I'd absorb them, well, at the most in five minutes. I look. I absorb. I go on.

BAR-MAN. Your method of absorption is not a reverent absorption.

MIRIAM. An adequate absorption.

BAR-MAN. You may think so, but.

MIRIAM. Reverence is a thing I am happy to leave in the hands of the reverent.

BAR-MAN. Will your husband go with you?

MIRIAM. No. It would take him an hour to absorb a pagoda.

BAR-MAN. Some that go to Kyoto sit before a pagoda all day and then all night. Reverence.

MIRIAM. Or pretension.—Has a woman ever held you with?

BAR-MAN. In our country the man prefers to hold our delicate ladies.

MIRIAM. Delicate ladies like dolls.

BAR-MAN. Delicate ladies with delicate manners and gestures.

MIRIAM. Oh, I've seen how they move. *(He comes from behind the bar with a tray of drinks.)* The venerable diplomats are going to fall under their tables.

BAR-MAN. Not unless there is a tremor, a quake of the earth. *(He exits D. R.)*

MIRIAM. That boy moves well, yes, he knows how to move. I'm sorry he has a position that ties him down. Otherwise, I'd not be going to Kyoto alone. Oh, well. I'll not be lonely. I know the word for hello. *(To audience.)* At a country club dance on Long Island—oh, I'm popular on Long Island!—I was dancing with this attractive but inexperienced-looking young man—and I whispered in his ear: "Do you mind if I manipulate your genitals?"—Scared him out of. He said "Here?" as if he was in church. I said I'll step out for some air and you follow me out. Did he?—Hmmm.—You bet he did!—And I manipulated his genitals all right.—HMMM.—yaisses!—between a Cadillac and a—hmm—Cadillac.—Sure, we got into one.—Burrgh—Recollections are insufficient. I like present action. *(Bar-man returns D. R. with empty tray. Crosses to behind bar.)* Bar-man. You, Bar-man! *(He continues filling a tray of drinks behind the bar. She takes out of her handbag a little silver whistle and blows it shrilly.)* I use this to catch the attention of a cab when I'm in New York.

BAR-MAN. What is? Did you say—?

MIRIAM. Cab. A public conveyance.

BAR-MAN. I am not a public convenience. I do not respond to whistles.

MIRIAM. I would like you to get me a cablegram blank from the concierge with the unfortunate face.

BAR-MAN. I will get you a cablegram from the bell-captain and place it on the green table. *(He goes out arch R. She goes to arch, Bar-man returns.)* Pardon me. You are instructing my way.

MIRIAM. Do you mean obstructing?

BAR-MAN. Thank you. I mean obstructing. To deliver the cablegrams to you, I must request that you return to your table.

MIRIAM. If I return to my table, will you bring the cablegram to me?

BAR-MAN. I will place it in reach of.

MIRIAM. You must place it on my table.

BAR-MAN. I will place the cablegram where you can reach it— You are still instructing—I mean obstructing my way.

MIRIAM. He won that little encounter, but you can lose a lot of encounters and still wind up as the winner. He's put a book of cablegrams on that other. Bar-man, I asked for a cablegram and you've brought me a whole book of them.

BAR-MAN. Is that enough, or do you want several books?

MIRIAM. You thought I was going to send cables all over the world? *(She laughs boisterously.)* —Oh. Could you give me a pencil?

BAR-MAN. Yes. Only one pencil?

MIRIAM. Only one pencil will do at the present moment. *(Speaking aloud as she writes.)* Mr. Leonard Frisbie. World Galleries. New York. Dear Leonard. I'm sorry to tell you that Mark has suffered a total collapse of the nervous system. Hmmm. Mental and physical, too. With most situations I am able to cope but not this one. I mean not alone. Mark is your greatest painter. Please fly to Tokyo at once. Otherwise I will be forced to. Hmmm. Unless you arrive as quickly as. With love as ever and with desperate appeal. Miriam Conley. There, now. That should do it. Young man? Give the cablegram to the concierge. It has to go out at once.

BAR-MAN. I am instructed to stay in my position at the bar at this time of.

MIRIAM. Disregard your instructions. I will give you two hundred yen to take the cablegram to the concierge and tell him it has to go out immediately.

BAR-MAN. —Put the cablegram on another table and I will pick it up.

MIRIAM. You're afraid to come to my table?

BAR-MAN. When I come to your table you place your hand improperly on my body.

MIRIAM. Ha! Look. The two hundred yen.

BAR-MAN. Place the cablegram on another table and.

MIRIAM. The cablegram stays here.

BAR-MAN. Then you must take it to the concierge.

MIRIAM. A pagan idol with the propriety of. Another two hundred yen. *(The Bar-man comes from behind the bar and comes to a position that should be safely away from the table, extends his arm to its full length.)* You have to remove that cablegram from the table or there's no deal.

BAR-MAN. Throw it at me, please, with the four hundred yen.

MIRIAM. I'll be damned if I will. You come to the table and take the cablegram off it and the four hundred yen. *(After some hesitation he comes to the table. She immediately places her hand on his crotch.)* Stay a while. You have no real objection.

BAR-MAN. —It's.

MIRIAM. What?

BAR-MAN. In Tokyo women bathe us.

MIRIAM. An interesting, a very intriguing idea. When do you want a bath?

BAR-MAN. I have had my bath. Without indecency.

MIRIAM. But you stay by the table.

BAR-MAN. Four hundred yen is a large sum for delivering a cablegram to the concierge and your hand is.

MIRIAM. The hand of a woman who burns.

BAR-MAN. Yes.

MIRIAM. *(She releases him, gives him the money and cablegram.)* Here is the cablegram and the four hundred yen. *(He starts to bar, stops.)* What's the matter?

BAR-MAN. I forgot the direction. *(Exits through arch, R.)*

MIRIAM. *(To audience.)* I'm fully aware, of course, that there's no magical trick to defend me indefinitely from the hideous product of calendars, clocks, watches. However I've made a covenant with them. When, or the unexpected but always possible advent of incurable illness. *(She removes a tiny pill-box from her bag.)* A Regency snuff-box: Innocent-looking. It contains one pill, just one, but the one is enough. When then. I will carry it into a grove of afternoon trees. Swallow the. And in a single, immeasurable moment— *(Bar-man returns.)* Did you?

BAR-MAN. The cablegram is.

MIRIAM. Thank you. I hope the evening train leaves before the light fades away. *(Wind chimes. The woman's husband enters* R. *He is her age but ravaged-looking. There are vivid paint stains on his un-pressed suit.)*

MARK. No chair for me at the table.

MIRIAM. You weren't expected. *(He attempts to draw a chair to the table but stumbles to his knees: staggers up with an apologetic laugh.)*

MARK. Too soon after work.

MIRIAM. Much.

MARK. I was fraid you'd.

MIRIAM. I wasn't waiting for you.

MARK. I'm glad I came down in time.

MIRIAM. Time for what?

MARK. To find you.

MIRIAM. Infantile dependence.

MARK. The work is.

MIRIAM. I'm not going to discuss it. You're leaning on the table for support, crouched over it.

MARK. It's always been exhausting to. Bar-man, yes, please.

MIRIAM. The manager of the hotel has complained of the paint stains on the floor of your room.

MARK. I covered the floor with several sheets of newspaper before I.

MIRIAM. The paint from the spray guns obviously goes through them.

MARK. If there are stains, I scrub them out with turpentine.

MIRIAM. Not well enough, it seems.

MARK. If I damage the floor of the room, I'll pay for a new one.

MIRIAM. Why not rent a loft to work in?

MARK. Where?

MIRIAM. Somewhere. A loft that has a window.

MARK. The time getting to a loft.

MIRIAM. Yes?

MARK. Would probably be too long to hold an image.

MIRIAM. The images of your new work must be extremely.

MARK. No, not at all. They're so vivid they.

MIRIAM. You could hire a car with a chauffeur and a siren to.

MARK. Miriam, don't ridicule the. *(The Bar-man places a cocktail before Mark. His hand is too tremulous to lift the glass to his mouth. He laughs breathlessly.)*

MIRIAM. If you can't lift the glass, put the hand not holding it under the elbow of. Oh, too late, now, you've spilt it. *(The Bar-man impassively wipes the table.)* Mr. Conley is.

BAR-MAN. I see. I know.

MIRIAM. Mix another for him, I'll pour it down him. His hands are.

BAR-MAN. Nerveless a little.

MARK. I've always been excited by work. But this time the excitement and the tension are. *(The Bar-man serves him another cocktail and returns to the bar, leaving the shaker on table.)*

MIRIAM. Don't touch it. I'll lift it to your mouth. *(She does.)* Your teeth are *chattering*— More?

MARK. Yes, all of it, please.

MIRIAM. Don't bite the glass. Open your mouth wider. Now. *(He chokes a little.)* That's all of it.

MARK. Thanks. I'd better have another.

BAR-MAN. There is another in the shaker.

MIRIAM. I'd better lift this one, too. Now. Mouth open wide. I said wide. If you're not the man in the side-show that swallows glass. This is.

MARK. Ridiculous of me.

BAR-MAN. Nerveless.

MARK. It's hard to come downstairs immediately after work.

MIRIAM. Yes. Apparently so.

MARK. Do you know how I. *(Laughs breathlessly.)* Move in my room?

MIRIAM. I think it's difficult for you to move anywhere.

MARK. I catch hold of a chair. I catch hold of the bureau. I catch hold of.

MIRIAM. How do you get to the elevator?

MARK. By. *(Laughs breathlessly.)* By leaning onto the wall. Stumbling along it.

MIRIAM. Would you go to a doctor if I found one for you?

MARK. All I could tell him is that the tension of my work.

MIRIAM. He might want to test your reflexes.

MARK. For the first time, primary colors and no. No technique that sep, sep!

MIRIAM. Are you trying to say separates?

MARK. Yes, separates, holds at some dis!

MIRIAM. To translate your incoherence, holds at some distance, is that it?

MARK. You understand what I'm trying to say.

MIRIAM. Maybe that, yes, but not what you're doing. Don't touch me with those stained fingers. Don't crouch and lean forward, try to sit straight in the chair. When I looked in your room and saw you crawling naked over a huge nailed-down canvas, I thought "My God, it's time for the."

MARK. I've understood the *intimacy* that should, that has to exist between the, the—painter and the—I! It! Now it turned to me, or I turned to it, no division between us at all anymore! The oneness, the!

MIRIAM. Are you hysterical?

MARK. I always stripped myself naked in my studio in.

MIRIAM. I'll get the bell-captain to get you a tape-recorder to preserve your delirious ravings. Play them back to yourself and you might be as shocked as I am by the.

MARK. Images in!

MIRIAM. Recorded.

MARK. There was always a sense of division till! Gone! Now absolute oneness with!

MIRIAM. You're shaking the table so that I have to grip the other side of it and try to keep it from.

MARK. *(He leans back.)* If I said that I'm.

MIRIAM. What?

MARK. Actually *terrified* of. Would you believe me?

MIRIAM. I have no reason to doubt it.

MARK. Excited, yes, *wildly*, but *terrified* at the same time, I.

MIRIAM. Mark.

MARK. This work is hard to confine to.

MIRIAM. Wants to run out, does it?

MARK. Always before I felt controllable limits, I.

MIRIAM. Shaking, unbathed, unshaved, blotches of paint in your hair. Look at yourself in this mirror if you're not blind. *(She holds her large mirror but he stares above it at her.)* Yes. *(Puts mirror on table.)* Blind.

MARK. Sometimes the interruption of work, especially in a new style, causes a, causes a—loss of momentum that's never recovered!

MIRIAM. Mark, fly back and.

MARK. If I, you'd fly back with me? Naturally you'd.

MIRIAM. No, Mark, I wouldn't.

MARK. You want me to?

MIRIAM. Deliver yourself to the loving care of your Aunt Grace who dotes on human catastrophes. I've never been around her more than two minutes before she says "Oh, do you know that so-and-so passed away or has had his spinal column removed." And of course you'd have Leonard's unlimited understanding. They'd meet you at the airport. They'd see your condition. It's their problem from there. I won't let it be mine.

MARK. Miriam, you don't mean you want me to fly back alone.

MIRIAM. No, not alone, with a nurse, and under heavy sedation, an oxygen mask, the whole bit, you wouldn't even be conscious that you were.

MARK. I can't interrupt my work here before I've controlled it.

MIRIAM. Mark, to be honest with you, the canvasses that I was privileged to look at.

MARK. Prematurely.

MIRIAM. Were circus-colored mud-pies.

MARK. That was in the beginning.

MIRIAM. Recently.

MARK. There's something so organic!

MIRIAM. Yes, I'll have the bell-captain get you a tape recorder.

MARK. I feel as if I were crossing the frontier of a country I have no permission to enter, but I enter, this, this! I tell you, it *terrifies* me! Now! In the beginning.

MIRIAM. Let it rest. At least, don't inflict the. Mark, it's not too late for surroundings familiar to you.

MARK. The drink was a mistake. Excuse me a moment.

MIRIAM. Indefinitely.

MARK. While I stick a finger down my throat. *(He exits* D. R.*)*

MIRIAM. Yes. Well. Gone. This goddam flower disturbs me. I can't stand it on the table. I can't say why, but sometimes a harmless object can disturb me enormously, yes, like that sunburst diamond pin of. "Sally, that pin is beautiful, but would you please take it off and." "Why, Miriam?" "I'm sorry, I can't say why." "All right, dear. I'll put it in my bag." "Thank you, Sally. Would you put the bag out of sight?" I learned a few days later that she thought I'd gone mad. And now this goddam flower must go. Could the reason be that a *cut* flower is unavoidably a *dying* flower? I'll ask him to remove it from the table.—Young man? Bar-man?

BAR-MAN. What is it?

MIRIAM. This flower on the table, will you please remove it?

BAR-MAN. Why?

MIRIAM. Because—I don't like objects that disguise their true nature, and there is nothing on earth that disguises its true nature more cunningly than a flower, even when cut and stuck in a vase in a bar.

BAR-MAN. If I have understood you, what is the true nature of?

MIRIAM. Rapacious. You know that word?

BAR-MAN. I think you have taught me that word.

MIRIAM. *(Rising and crossing toward bar.)* Maybe a stronger word is ravenous.

BAR-MAN. Do you mean you are a flower?

MIRIAM. You know what I am.

BAR-MAN. I have had—am I speaking correctly?

MIRIAM. Yes. Continue. Go on with.

BAR-MAN. On our island which is too small for its habitations?

MIRIAM. Inhabitants.

BAR-MAN. Thank you. We prefer flowers to.

MIRIAM. *(Smiling, she crosses to her chair and sits.)* You had an idiomatic expression in your mind.

BAR-MAN. I believe the word is ancient and universal.

MIRIAM. *(She picks up flower and gives it to him.)* Here. Not wanted.

BAR-MAN. Oh?

MIRIAM. No.

BAR-MAN. I have been instructed to be sure that a vase containing a flower is on each table. The purple flower on the red table is. *(Returning the vase and flower to her table.)*

MIRIAM. Not wanted by a hotel guest in the bar. *(Handing the Bar-man vase and flower.)*

BAR-MAN. Before your trip to Kyoto, you might, may, would enjoy a long stroll about the garden of the hotel.

MIRIAM. There is something you "might, may, would" enjoy, too.

BAR-MAN. Thank you. No. Madam Flower. *(The Bar-man replaces vase and flower on table. Picks up shaker and Mark's glass and returns to bar.)*

MIRIAM. Crock. *(Mark staggers back to the table. Miriam rises.)* I'll get a bell-boy to help you back to your room.

MARK. No, no, no. I'm afraid to go in it again.

MIRIAM. Then go in my room. Here's my key. Throw that fantastically decorated suit out the window, take a shower, have the bell-boy bring you a clean suit, if you have one, and.

MARK. When I say that I'm terrified of the new canvasses, you think I'm exaggerating.

MIRIAM. Not at all in the least.

MARK. No separation between myself and.

MIRIAM. Don't keep repeating it to me. Saying a thing once to me is enough, you know. Sometimes a thing doesn't even have to be said to me. I'm able to guess it.

MARK. It's something that.

MIRIAM. I said "Don't discuss it." Not outside the office of a.

MARK. In the beginning, a new style of work can be stronger than you, but you learn to control it. It has to be controlled. You learn to control it.

MIRIAM. Fly back immediately.

MARK. I always suspected that tigers were hiding in.

MIRIAM. *(Sits in her chair.)* It's not a question of whether you want to or not, it's something you've got to face as something that's.

MARK. Fly back?

MIRIAM. Yes. Imperative. At once. I've suggested to you, I've urged you to follow, the. More? I can't do more. Yes, I could do more. I could have you put in a sanitarium here. I could, and I will if you force me. I'm right. Bar-man, a.

MARK. Yes. One for me, too.

MIRIAM. Mr. Conley will have a *Coca-Cola*. For God's sake, Mark, you must have noticed your loss of balance. Why, your stumbling into things is. And you admit how you move around in your room.

MARK. An artist has to lay his life on the line.

MIRIAM. Once I dreamed that the shy, gifted man that you were would lift me above the trivialties in my life. I took the initiative and didn't mind taking it. Mark, I said, why don't we go somewhere together, married or not married.

MARK. A friend of yours loaned you.

MIRIAM. His yacht. The shy, gifted man said the bunks are too narrow for two. I'll take the upper, good night. Hell. OK. I mounted the ladder to the upper bunk, and I lay on the body of a secret vendor of silk.

MARK. You were remarkably skilled in overcoming timidity.

MIRIAM. Had to be or no show.

MARK. Afterwards we went up on the deck and I pointed out to you.

MIRIAM. Stars and constellations. You could name them. Oh and the Northern Lights that night they made a crackling sound like giant white sheets being shaken out in the sky.

MARK. While I fondled your breasts, as I still desperately long to.

MIRIAM. Mark, your hands are.

MARK. I know, I know—I know.

MIRIAM. Your condition has to be diagnosed by a good neuropathologist, soon as. Immediately.

MARK. Miriam, I swear it's the intensity of.

MIRIAM. If you're going to discuss the intensity of your new work, sit at that other table and discuss it with yourself.

MARK. Why did you say a neuro-pathologist?

MIRIAM. I had an uncle that had a brain tumor and the symptoms were identical.

MARK. I'm not going to interrupt my.

MIRIAM. Well, take a loft with a window.

MARK. The images flash in my brain, and I have to get them on nailed-down canvas at once or they.

MIRIAM. Flash back out of your brain. A neuropathologist would be interested in that. I'm not a neuropathologist and I'm not concerned with a thing about this thing but flying you into the care of.

MARK. There's a feeling of, a sense of.

MIRIAM. You won't shut up about it.

MARK. Of, of.

MIRIAM. Stop it.

MARK. Adventuring into a jungle country with wild men crouching in bushes, in in, in—trees, with poison arrows to.

MIRIAM. Yes, to kill you, and they've nearly done it. *(The Bar-man has served the drink and the Coca-Cola.)*

MARK. Color.

MIRIAM. That's right. Color. On your suit, your hands, even in your hair.

MARK. I didn't know it till now. Color, color, and light! Before us and after us, too. What I'm saying is—color isn't passive, it, it—has a fierce life in it!

MIRIAM. This sort of talk isn't suitable to a public room in a.

MARK. The possibilities of color and light, discovered all at once, can make a man fall on the street. I've heard that finally on earth there'll be nothing but gigantic insects but now I know the last things, the imperishable things, are color and light. Finished. No more about it. I won't fly back to New York with a nurse under heavy sedation.

MIRIAM. I could have you committed.

MARK. It wouldn't be the first time you've tried to put me away, without.

MIRIAM. Without what?

MARK. Without considering the.

MIRIAM. What?

MARK. The consequences. I never could stand confinement.

MIRIAM. When a person needs help.

MARK. I.

MIRIAM. Yes. You. What?

MARK. There were.

MIRIAM. There were what?

MARK. Several times when I suspected, when I knew you despised me.

MIRIAM. Paranoia.

MARK. Don't say that.

MIRIAM. I say what I see when it needs to be—has to be said.

MARK. Let's make a bargain, Miriam. You fly back with me. And we'll go to Long Island and I'll, I'll—I'll take the chance of the interruption.

MIRIAM. Oh, no, that's no acceptable bargain.

MARK. Sometimes, what was it, the work I've done, but a good preparation for.

MIRIAM. You've always had styles of your own but it's not what you're doing now by a rocket shot to the moon.

MARK. What I'm doing now is.

MIRIAM. If you take a shower, odious as a shower's become to you lately, you can sleep off your exhaustion in the twin bed by the door in my room.

BAR-MAN. Mr. Conley is nerveless.

MIRIAM. You keep saying nerveless for nervous,

BAR-MAN. Pardon, please.

MIRIAM. *(Speaking quietly to Mark, her head turned away from the Bar-man.)* While you were sticking a finger down your throat, there was a controversy between me and that impertinent Bar-man.

MARK. Over?

MIRIAM. Over the flower on the table. Do you think you could remove the flower and vase and explain to the Bar-man, who seems to understand you better than he does me, that I will not share a small table with that purple flower.

MARK. —Yes, of course, but I.

MIRIAM. You know how some objects.

MARK. —Yes. I'll simply put it on the bar and say that my wife hates flowers.

MIRIAM. Say that *you* hate them too. *(He crosses toward bar and falls to his knees before it.)*

BAR-MAN. Did you injure yourself, Mr. Conley?

MARK. I—hate flowers.

BAR-MAN. I don't think it is you. Let me help you to.

MARK. Thank you, yes, please.

BAR-MAN. A beautiful flower has to be on each table.

MARK. Please help me back to the table, and explain to my wife. *(Mark moves slowly, stops the Bar-man from helping him. He reaches Miriam, swings at her hat, misses. She rises and he takes her seat. The Bar-man places the vase and flower on the table.)*

MIRIAM. *(Facing front and speaking as if to herself.)* The disguised rapacity of a flower means nothing to me. It doesn't offer the least. No. In Wetherbridge the woman next door, Sally, said to me, "Miriam, you cut too many flowers and yet I've never seen flowers in your house. Do you contribute the flowers to hospitals or?" I told her the truth. I said, "No, I contribute them to the incinerator." She went "Heh-heh." There is a lot of difference between going heh-heh and going ha-ha. Heh-heh is an expression of nervous confusion, which I've never had, but ha-ha expresses genuine amusement. Flower, you're cut and you'll die. The sentence of death is imposed on you, purple flower. *(To Mark.)* Yesterday, on the Ginzah, I ran into an old schoolmate from Silver Hall, Elaine. We're lunching together and she said strictly no husbands. I think she wants to discuss what's called a marital problem.

MARK. When? How much time is?

MIRIAM. I said that she said no husbands.

MARK. I could sit at a different table till the discussion of the marriage problem is.

MIRIAM. Even if I weren't having lunch with Elaine I wouldn't with you today.

MARK. I have an immaculately clean summer suit.

MIRIAM. It would do nothing for your disequilibrium on the.

MARK. After a quick, cold shower, I.

MIRIAM. You don't hear what I say. It's useless talking to you.

MARK. The loss of balance comes from the.

MIRIAM. I said that she said that.

MARK. I can't be left alone now.

MIRIAM. You have your primary colors.

MARK. I have a clean summer suit and after a cold shower, I.

MIRIAM. For God's sake, can't I be allowed some freedom of?

MARK. Yes, of course. It's only that.

MIRIAM. Tyrannical dependence.

MARK. I'm sorry. It's all right. It's just that.

MIRIAM. If you need a hired companion. You're sitting on my coat. Bar-man, call me a cab.

MARK. I'll have a little lunch here. *(Rises.)* Or maybe I would be able to sleep awhile in your room.

MIRIAM. Visit the galleries of Tokyo.

MARK. I'm afraid it's true that.

MIRIAM. Work that isn't your own.

MARK. Disturbs me. Yes. Even when I admire it.

MIRIAM. You must reconcile yourself to the fact that some paintings you haven't painted will.

MARK. Exist in the world. Yes.

MIRIAM. Visit the galleries of Tokyo.

MARK. The work is so intense, it.

MIRIAM. You wanted the work, you took the work, you're stuck with it.

MARK. I also took a woman to be my wife.

MIRIAM. The woman has her own existence, doesn't she? Did you call me a cab?

BAR-MAN. There are cabs waiting outside the door.

MARK. Your friend would understand, if.

MIRIAM. She said as I said strictly no husbands, meaning none in any condition.

MARK. I've always approached my work with a feeling of.

MIRIAM. Yes?

MARK. Of frightened timidity because the possibilities are.

MIRIAM. You are making an effort to explain a mystery that I.

MARK. The possibilities of a canvas that presents itself for. To be romantic about it, which I've always been, is to. I have to recognize that to doubt is necessary.

MIRIAM. I have to leave in a minute.

MARK. It's exhausting but—I suppose I might say that.

MIRIAM. You're destroying.

MARK. I suppose I might say that.

MIRIAM. Crock.

MARK. Adventure.

MIRIAM. *(Crosses to* C. *table, putting cigarettes and lighter into her bag.)* Well, Mark, you and your spray guns and your primary colors will have to do without me several days when I go to Kyoto.

MARK. I'll.

MIRIAM. You'll stay here with your work.

MARK. —It could be a fantasy that I'm.

MIRIAM. Shattering a frontier?

MARK. *(Crosses to* R. *arch.)* In my room is a suit I've never worn. A shower takes me two minutes. I'll be down in five.

MIRIAM. I won't be seen today with a man that.

MARK. I've always felt that. After the work, so little is left of me. To give to another person.

MIRIAM. Mark.

MARK. Miriam.

MIRIAM. Go back to the States. Enter a. Consult a. As your wife, I.

MARK. I can't interrupt the.

MIRIAM. I have clipped flowers outside your studio and heard you talk to your work as if you were talking to another person in the studio with you.

MARK. No. To myself.

MIRIAM. And I was clipping flowers. It's natural that I.

MARK. Felt?

MIRIAM. Sometimes a little excluded, but I never spoke of it, did I?

MARK. The work of a painter is lonely.

MIRIAM. So is clipping flowers. I'm afraid that loneliness has become a worn-out thing to discuss.

MARK. No more mention of it. But, for God's sake, don't go to Kyoto without me.

MIRIAM. I am going to Kyoto and I am not going with you. You'll return to the States and you will consult a.

MARK. He would only tell me what I already know. You know there isn't much further.

MIRIAM. Your least attractive quality is self-pity.

MARK. I was being objective.

MIRIAM. Tell the concierge, he understands and speaks English, that you need someone, that you need an art student to take you about the galleries of Tokyo. Of course, shave, bathe, and dress first.

MARK. When I heard you clipping flowers outside my studio, it would sometimes occur to me that you wished the flowers you were clipping were my.

MIRIAM. What's become of the man that?

MARK. What's become of the woman that?

MIRIAM. I'm usually tolerant of men that are unknown to me, but you've become one.

MARK. The constant unbearable of.

MIRIAM. *Mine!*

MARK. *Mine!*—Did you really think I was sleeping night after goddam night when you slipped out of your bed and threw on a coat over you? Did you think I didn't hear you starting your car that you never put in the garage but left in front of the house? How many kinds of a fool do you take me for? Every? ALL? And near daybreak, did you think I didn't hear you coming back? Sometimes the hanger dropping in the closet? Your slipping demurely back into your bed, your, your satisfied sighs of?

MIRIAM. Assuming.

MARK. *Knowing!*

MIRIAM. Assuming—

MARK. I said knowing, and you know that I knew!

MIRIAM. You never—

MARK. Spoke of it to you? No!

MIRIAM. —Why?

MARK. I said to myself—

MIRIAM. What did you say to yourself? Something or nothing?

MARK. She offers the compliment to me of waiting until she thinks that I'm asleep. *(Wind chimes.)*

MIRIAM. —Are we two people, Mark, or are we—

MARK. *(With the force of dread.)* Stop there! *(She lifts her hands to her face, but the words continue through it.)*

MIRIAM. Two sides of!

MARK. Stop!

MIRIAM. One! An artist inhabiting the body of a compulsive—

MARK. Bitch!

MIRIAM. Call me that, but remember that you're denouncing a side of yourself, denied by you! And remember this, too. You'd enter my bed at daybreak, and tired as I was, I never refused myself to you. The vendor of silk that was secret! I probably knew that he knew.

MARK. *(Cutting through her line above.)* Give me the five minutes, all I need, to look proper for this occasion.

MIRIAM. None, not one.

MARK. Go on, you cunt, to this, this—lunch with a gentleman named Elaine. I'm sure you'll be on time. You won't keep him waiting, this gentleman named Elaine with his marital difficulties. You'll give him invaluable counsel. And I, as for me, the man that you married is still a living man with no broken bones, and if later on I feel hungry, I'll have lunch alone, but not in my room with canvasses demanding what I can't give them yet, no, but as for Kyoto, bitch, we'll go there together, or. *(He seizes her shoulders, she staggers to her knees, he lifts her and flings her through the arch, out of the bar.)*

BAR-MAN. —Mr. Conley, do you want to be assisted to your room?

MARK. *(Crossing to C. table, sits in chair.)* I think that I will stay here till my wife returns from. *(The stage is dimmed out.)*

PART II

The Bar-man, jacket open, is washing glasses in a cloud of steam. Miriam enters through arch.

BAR-MAN. The bar is not open.

MIRIAM. It's open when I come in. *(The Hawaiian Lady enters* R. *arch and exits* D. R.*)* The bed has been repaired! And I see you're putting the vase with the flower back on my table. OK. Hmm. Your jacket is open today. Becoming.

BAR-MAN. The bar is not open until twelve o'clock and I am washing glasses in hot water. The steam may paralyze you.

MIRIAM. There's no danger of that. I'll tell you something I've noticed about Japanese men. On their bodies, as a usual thing, they have almost no hair.

BAR-MAN. You have investigated?

MIRIAM. Yes, I've conducted some little investigations that aren't in a travel book. I don't like hairy men. I like men to have just the essential hair on their bodies. In their armpits and over their sexual organs. More than that? No. Permissible, sometimes, but essential never. I'll have a French 75 to celebrate the.

BAR-MAN. You'll have a what?

MIRIAM. I was just putting you on—

BAR-MAN. Putting me on what?

MIRIAM. I'll have a stinger.

BAR-MAN. The bar is closed until.

MIRIAM. You've been too busy to look at the clock. It says three minutes to twelve, and by the time you've mixed a stinger for me, if you know how to mix one, it will be twelve or after.

BAR-MAN. A stinger is made with gin and?

MIRIAM. I think I'd better mix it myself. *(She goes back of the bar and he goes in front of it with noticeable rapidity.)* You've got the ingredients, but you don't know the mix. And you sure did get out of here on the double quick when I got in with you.

BAR-MAN. You have delayed your trip to Kyoto.

MIRIAM. I have some little business matters to settle here before absorbing Kyoto.

BAR-MAN. You should absorb the Izu Peninsula.

MIRIAM. *(Remaining behind the bar.)* Hmmm. What is there to absorb there?

BAR-MAN. Very beautiful sights of the sea, and the restful hot springs.

MIRIAM. Oh? So. I've mixed my stinger. Equal parts of brandy and creme de menthe. Green or white. Remember that and remember me as the lady that taught you that.

BAR-MAN. I doubt that this particular instruction is all that would prevent?

MIRIAM. Yes, prevent.

BAR-MAN. My remembering that you spent a little time here. Will you please to take your drink to your table now.

MIRIAM. You're supposed to take the drinks to the tables.

BAR-MAN. I know that I am, and I have told you that I am engaged and not faithless.

MIRIAM. Yes, you did tell me that. Hmm. I haven't forgotten that sad bit of information. But despite it. I've known very few men that I couldn't surprise a little.

BAR-MAN. Go to Kyoto. Go to Kyoto today.

MIRIAM. Oh, I'll go to Kyoto. *(She returns with drink above her table.)* Lovely old pagodas with clear pools to reflect them and the flowering trees in flower. Perhaps after that I'll absorb the Izu Peninsula with you.

BAR-MAN. I have steady employment.

MIRIAM.

"Never worry, never fear,
Someday you'll meet a rich old queer."

A recent addition to the Mother Goose book. Hmmm. Yes. Konnichiwa. That's the word for hello. Hong Kong. Singapore. Bangkok—what a name for a city! Hmmm. I think I'll skip India where on the streets they drop dead of starvation. Misfortunes don't attract me. *(Buzzer sounds.)*

BAR-MAN. Pardon me. I am called to the restaurant. *(He exits. A middle-aged man who looks younger enters the circle of light.)*

LEONARD. I like your costume.

MIRIAM. Do you think I cabled you that it was desperately urgent for you to fly from New York to Tokyo in order for you to make a comment on what I'm wearing?

LEONARD. I spent an hour with him. A painter with Mark's talent and originality is a restless creature that lives in his private jungle.

MIRIAM. Crock.

LEONARD. He doesn't work for the purpose of having a price tag in four figures on his paintings.

MIRIAM. More crock. Is that all I'm going to get from you?

LEONARD. Of course I'm stalling. If I said that I've never seen so much torment expressed in canvasses before, your response would be crock, I suppose. *(She hurls the flower vase at the bar.)*

MIRIAM. There. That's my response.

LEONARD. Violence isn't an element missing from your nature. Let's consider a little.

MIRIAM. I've considered all I'm going to consider, but how did you like his room?

LEONARD. His room, when he let me in it, well, it. I understood the urgency of your cable, yes, I. But, Miriam, it's the physical thing, his physical condition that mainly disturbed me, and I'm sure it.

MIRIAM. It disturbs the people he crashes into on the street, too.

LEONARD. Yes, I.

MIRIAM. Mark made his reputation as an adventurous. Now I'll tell you something that'll give you a turn and a twist, just dig this. He thinks he's made the discovery, the first discovery, of color.

LEONARD. Well, of course, there's always been some question as to whether or not color existed before there were eyes to see it.

MIRIAM. Crock! Don't make cornball remarks, pseudo-philosophical cornball remarks like that to me that Mark's made to you.

LEONARD. I was merely.

MIRIAM. Yes, merely. Mark thinks he's discovered color and he's terrified of it. Says it's glorious but is terrified of it. How does that grab you or does it just bounce off you?

LEONARD. Painters must be allowed.

MIRIAM. You didn't hear me. I said he's *terrified* of it.

LEONARD. That, he told me that, too.

MIRIAM. You take him back to. His dependence on me is like a baby and a baby is something I never wanted, *never*!

LEONARD. Not so loud.

MIRIAM. I want you to hear me, Leonard.

LEONARD. Your intentions, what are they?

MIRIAM. Not continuing with him and not returning with him.

LEONARD. I thought you cared for Mark?

MIRIAM. Whom else have I spent a considerable part of my life with? But I'm not going to deprive myself of this trip. And there's a reason I won't, and I won't. And there's a reason.

LEONARD. Your desertion of him.

MIRIAM. There are sedations, stretchers, planes and.

LEONARD. Yes. Well, I see. I'll get some plane schedules and. *(He exits through arch.)*

MIRIAM. Some women grow suddenly old. They go to bed young, well, reasonably young women and when they wake up in the morning and go to the mirror, they face—what?—A spectre! Yes, they face a spectre! Themselves, yes, but not young, reasonably young, women, no, not anymore! Oh, they continue to pursue, if they are like me, the pursuit would continue! But the desired stranger would offer them no more than a minute of his time. A glance in a glistening bar. And I fear death, I know it would have to remove, wrench, tear!—the bracelets off my arms. Insignia of attraction still persisting. Then? In solitude, in a grove of afternoon trees or the bedroom of a hotel, the mortal pill-box—held still in reserve. To be old, suddenly old—*no!* Unacceptable to me on any terms. So I wait in dread. Terror, yes, I could say terror! *(She wrenches her brilliant bracelets up and down on her arms.)* No inner resources of serenity in me at all. A woman burning. Nothing to put the flames out. A woman condemned to the stake and. Oh, but that's later on. *(Leonard returns.)* Excuse me, Leonard. I was thinking of something…

LEONARD. I was looking at schedules of planes, but frankly, Miriam, all your friends will be shocked.

MIRIAM. Tell them to go to Kyoto. And you, don't give me an argument about it. This trip, Leonard, has a special importance to me that, that I won't try to explain or justify or.

LEONARD. If you intend to.

MIRIAM. Back he goes to the States in your care, Leonard.

LEONARD. Who will finance your?

MIRIAM. Sometimes his dependence on me has been convenient. *(She removes a black leather case from her handbag: opens it.)*

LEONARD. Letter of credit for.

MIRIAM. Exactly. Made out in my name. He goes in a sanitarium and I continue as planned. Set free. Unencumbered. I love hotels. Room-service in them and bars. I choose my choice.

LEONARD. Abandonment, at a time when.

MIRIAM. I have, under my own name, in Morgan Manhattan Storage, about, no less than two hundred of his best paintings before he discovered color with spray guns, and I also have a hell of a lot of his drawings.

LEONARD. You are a practical woman with an eye for.

MIRIAM. Any contingency, yes. *(The Bar-man enters* D. R.*, crosses* L.*, notices vase and flower on the floor, picks them up, places on* C. *table and crosses behind bar.)*

LEONARD. Yes, of course, I know that. Bar-man, I would like.

MIRIAM. Mark will ask you to exhibit this stuff. Oh, he will. What'll you say to that?

LEONARD. I'll say "Mark, not yet."

MIRIAM. Well, he would have it exhibited in another gallery that would exhibit it because of his name.

LEONARD. That, I don't believe that.

MIRIAM. Don't believe it, Leonard, but I have an unalterable plan.

The man is mad. He is mad!

LEONARD. Are you speaking of?

MIRIAM. Mark! Yes, Mark! I'm speaking of.

LEONARD. I wouldn't.

MIRIAM. You wouldn't but I would! You see the completed pictures, you never hear him at work. I do. I've heard him shout at the studio canvas. "You bitch, it's *you* or *me*! I'm getting, I've got you now! A burst of light in the."

LEONARD. Miriam, not so loud.

MIRIAM. I'd send the maid out at three or four with some food. "Get the fuck out of!" Once he struck with the tray! You! You see the completed paintings. I? I hear the continual madness of his attack on the canvasses as he paints, and I can say with authority on the. Mark is mad! I am married to *madness*! I need some space between myself and.—A man raging in dark! Constantly further away from. *(A tinkling of glass chimes.)*

LEONARD. *(Seeing Mark in R. arch.)* He's come down.

MIRIAM. Oh, God, I'm not going to look at him. Where's he standing?

LEONARD. I pretended not to see him. He's obviously ashamed of.

MIRIAM. He's past shame.

LEONARD. He's leaning against the wall, not looking at us.

MIRIAM. Covered with paint?

LEONARD. He's shaved and cut his face but he has on a clean summer suit. I'm looking at him from the corner of my eye.

MIRIAM. Let's go out in the garden, before he crashes into the table. *(Mark exits.)*

LEONARD. He's going into the lavatory to get off his face the blood.

MIRIAM. A primary color. A man that stinks like a goat and staggers into everything he.

LEONARD. He took a shower and fell on the shower floor. Caught hold of the shower curtains and tore them off the rod.

MIRIAM. If you value his past work, tell him it's necessary for him to go back to the States immediately.

LEONARD. No plane of any airline out of Tokyo would accept him as a passenger.

MIRIAM. On a stretcher under heavy sedation.

LEONARD. A doctor would have to sign a slip, a certification, that Mark is fit to travel, and I don't think a doctor would.

MIRIAM. What do you suggest, then?

LEONARD. He might be accepted as a passenger on a ship: That's all that I can suggest.

MIRIAM. Leonard? There's a limit to things and I want out.

LEONARD. You mean? Without you?

MIRIAM. Yes, I'm going to follow the plan I planned.

LEONARD. His dependence on you is.

MIRIAM. Yes and on you.

LEONARD. Do you mean that, in spite of his complete dependence on you, you would consider?

MIRIAM. I don't want to spend my life with my feet in blocks of cement.

LEONARD. Miriam, I operate a gallery, I'm not a divorce attorney.

MIRIAM. The idea of the ship back to the States.

LEONARD. An excellent idea, but he'd have to accept it.

MIRIAM. I'm his wife. Temporarily. Any divorce lawyer would.

LEONARD. My gallery has exhibited the work of painters that painted with their toes. We even have one that paints with his penis.

MIRIAM. Erect or soft?

LEONARD. We are used to extremes. Our gallery is used to, you might say partial, to extremes of.

MIRIAM. To resurrect an old idiom, isn't that fine and dandy? Hmmm. Mark hasn't shown any marked preference for figurative or conventional styles of. He's gone through drip, fling, sopped, stained, saturated, scraped, ripped, cut, skeins of, mounds of heroically enduring color, but now he's arrived at a departure that's a real departure that I doubt he'll return from. Oh, I'm no fool about the. His sacred studio, talking to his. And his black and white period before he.

LEONARD. The, uh, the very early, exploratory phase of a new technique is not for exhibition, and that's what I told him. He took it well. He agreed. But most of the time I was holding him on his feet. I wish you would understand the seriousness of his. *(Miriam sees Mark off* D. R.*)*

MIRIAM. His face is covered with bloody tissue paper. When he comes to the table, if he can make it, I want you as his friend to tell him that. Leonard?

LEONARD. Yes.

MIRIAM. Why do you think I cabled you that he?

LEONARD. It isn't the extremes of. There are many wonderful ways to apply paint to canvas or wood or to a sheet of metal or slab of stone or.

MIRIAM. Leonard, I'm afraid I shouldn't have appealed to you.

LEONARD. Miriam, his chief concern right now is.

MIRIAM. Is?

LEONARD. A change that he feels or imagines in your attitude toward him. *(Mark enters* D. R. *and crosses to* C. *table, bloodied bits of tissue paper scattered over his face. He has on a clean white suit but has obviously lost weight so it doesn't fit him. His appearance is ravaged and fantastic: yet he has a childlike quality. When he speaks, his voice trembles.)*

MARK. Bar-man, another chair at the table, please, and. *(The Barman sets the chair at the table. Miriam looks straight ahead coldly. Mark starts to sit down but pitches forward, hard, against the table. He laughs breathlessly,)*

MIRIAM. There, now! How does this little demonstration of his public appearance and behavior impress you, if you can imagine yourself in my place? The embarrassment of it is!

LEONARD. He may be embarrassed as you are, and possibly more.

MIRIAM. He's not at all, not in the least embarrassed. Not a bit in the. Don't you hear him laughing?

LEONARD. He's laughing out of embarrassment.

MIRIAM. I'm sorry that I can't laugh out of disgust. If I could laugh out of disgust, it would be the biggest "Ha-ha" you've ever heard, but unfortunately—*stop it!*—my disgust doesn't amuse me at all in the least. And the incident isn't unusual, it's usual, and now are you able to understand why I say that I've *had* it? And *meant* it?

LEONARD. Your voice is.

MIRIAM. Never mind my voice.

LEONARD. Shouting about it is.

MIRIAM. Totally justified!

LEONARD. But, uh.

MIRIAM. *(First to Mark, then to Leonard.) Stop it*, stop it! And you, don't you say cool it, goddam if I'll cool it!

LEONARD. It does no good to exaggerate an incident that's painful to us all.

MIRIAM. Your sympathy for him is just a little abnormal, yes, just a little, always calling him baby. Well, here's your baby, take out adoption papers. No difficulty about it, no opposition.

LEONARD. I've learned to have to.

MIRIAM. OK, ignore, ignore.

LEONARD. Yes, ignore and forget.

MIRIAM. Space!

LEONARD. What about?

MIRIAM. Space between two people is sometimes.

LEONARD. *(To Mark.)* This, uh, these, uh, little attacks of, uh, disequilibrium have only troubled you recently, haven't they, Mark?

MARK. Since the. I knocked the breath out of. Let me get back my breath, and.

MIRIAM. Flying over here, he kept complaining that the plane cabins were not pressurized enough, and they were pressurized perfectly. *(They sit in silence a while as Mark struggles to catch his breath.)*

LEONARD. Mark, I think a. *(Mark nods.)* Bar-man, for Mr. Conley, please.

MIRIAM. Lots of luck, if you expect him to deliver a drink to this table.

MARK. I found, I put on a. *(Draws a difficult breath.)* Clean summer suit, but, you see, I forgot my.

LEONARD. What did you forget, Mark?

MARK. My electric razor in Wetherbridge.

LEONARD. I think that unconsciously we resent shaving. I've often made trips and forgotten my razor. But this time Raymond packed for me, so I have my electric razor. Of course you're welcome to use it.

MIRIAM. Very relevant to the.

LEONARD. *(Grateful for a light topic.)* The Japanese make such lovely, compact electric appliances, such as their Sony transistors, and their, their. *(He keeps glancing nervously at Mark.)* —Do you like my star sapphire?

MIRIAM. I think it's an appropriate adornment.

LEONARD. From Raymond on my birthday. *(Miriam snatches a small object from her handbag. Leonard's attitude during the snuff-box lines is detached, his attention remaining on Mark.)*

MIRIAM. How do you like my little Regency snuff-box?

LEONARD. Charming. *(She shakes it.)* You have something in it.

MIRIAM. Yes. Snuff.

LEONARD. Snuff doesn't rattle.

MIRIAM. It rattles when it's compressed.

LEONARD. Compressed snuff is something I've never heard of.

MIRIAM. Maybe you will. Snuff, snuff, enough.

MARK. I'll get my breath back.

LEONARD. Of course you will in a moment.—Miriam, Mark is a man of complexities that we.

MIRIAM. What an observation to make to a woman that's lived with him fourteen years.

MARK. If I imposed, I never meant to impose.

MIRIAM. Leonard, let's go straight to the point of your presence here in Japan.

MARK. I was.

LEONARD. What?

MARK. Always willing to.

LEONARD. What?

MARK. Die.

LEONARD. Mark means for you.

MIRIAM. He has a studio separate from the house, and as for dying for me, I prefer to have someone living for me, which I think is a natural preference.

MARK. The time.

LEONARD. It's twelve-fifteen.

MARK. Not what I meant. The time that you wait. To catch your breath, or *not* catch it.

MIRIAM. Nothing is being accomplished at this little round table conference.

MARK. The time you wait to recover. Or not to recover. And you're so revolted by the fear that you feel.

LEONARD. Fear is a built-in protection. Nothing to be ashamed of. I doubt that any living creature of the, the, uh, animal, mammal species isn't provided with it. Possibly fish don't have it. No, I think even fish are frightened when they're.

MIRIAM. You have a remarkable facility for keeping things at sea-level.

LEONARD. Sometimes it's the name of the game. Did the Bar-man make the?

MIRIAM. It's on the bar. Go get it.

LEONARD. The service in this bar is.

MIRIAM. No service.

LEONARD. *(Fetching the drink.)* Let me make a suggestion.

MIRIAM. Yes, do that. What is your suggestion?

LEONARD. —What an interminable plane-flight from New York to Tokyo, with all the changes in time. To repeat it immediately, I mean in reverse, would be a little too much.

MIRIAM. Is that your suggestion?

MARK. Yes. Interminable.

MIRIAM. You don't have to repeat it at once, you can have my room next to Mark's while I visit Kyoto.

LEONARD. Your intention is to?

MIRIAM. Catch the evening clackety-clack to Kyoto alone.

MARK. Something has.

LEONARD. What, Mark?

MARK. Affected my.

LEONARD. Affected your?

MARK. —Vision. Our breathing and the, the—pulsation of our, our—arteries are things that we are so used to that we usually don't think about them, but—

LEONARD. Yes. We take them for granted.

MARK. As permanent possessions, but they're only loaned to us, and the loan of.

LEONARD. Mark, baby, you simply.

MARK. Yes. Was simply reminded that breath in my. Is something not given but loaned, and the loan is.

LEONARD. We've all had the breath knocked out of us for a few moments.

MIRIAM. Yes, that's right, Mark, baby.

MARK. The loan is subject to, to—unexpected.

LEONARD. Don't try to get up till.

MARK. Foreclosure? Is that the way that?

LEONARD. It's not important, but rest here a little longer.

MARK. I will. Has she left the room?

LEONARD. No. She's still in the room.

MARK. I—like—this—room.—My breath is—coming back, now.

LEONARD. Good. Good.

MARK. I'll tell you something about what's called—the breath of life in us. No, I don't have the breath to tell you.

MIRIAM. I have a few things more to attend to before.

MARK. Miriam?

MIRIAM. I wanted to come here alone but he wouldn't allow me a little time of space between us, oh, no, he followed me here like the tin can that children tie to the tail of a cat in an alley.

LEONARD. Let's.

MIRIAM. Not upset Mark baby.

MARK. I'm beginning to feel all right. Perfectly. Have the razor cuts stopped bleeding?

LEONARD. Oh, yes, they've stopped bleeding, now.

MIRIAM. Comparatively.

MARK. *(Rises, is almost steady.)* Ladies and gentlemen pardon me… Lady and Leonard.

MIRIAM. He's decided to be offensive, now that he's got his breath back.

LEONARD. It's only the state of his.

MARK. You thought I was talking to you. I was talking to myself. A serious painter has two requirements—a long white beard and a—and a stepladder. *(Talking to himself.)* Mark you're talking about a thing that.

LEONARD. A thing that can't be clearly expressed at this point of.

MARK. Yep that's what you need to give you a constantly full quart of confidence in. A long white beard and a stepladder and a commission to paint—what did he paint on the ceiling of the Sistine Chapel.

LEONARD. Michelangelo painted the creation of the world on the ceiling of the.

MARK. The creation of the creation of the creation.

MIRIAM. Don't encourage him to. *(Mark staggers a little. Leonard touches his shoulder.)*

MARK. Don't touch me—I can't stand to be touched!

LEONARD. I can't believe that a painter's dependence on the wealth of the Church would please you. Would it, Mark, baby? No. I—

MARK. Crock, as the lady would put it. I'm anyone's whore, including my own. The lady—where is she? Oh, there she is!—Christ! She looks like a three-masted schooner today, billowing out of a harbor with a cargo of that stuff made from coconuts. Copra?

And a crew of some of them shanghaied, but the wind and the sea are favorable to her sailing around the Cape of, and if she's becalmed in equatorial waters she'll get the crew at the oars, oh, they'll row for the lady and live on hard tack.

MIRIAM. The hell with.

MARK. Suck my ass in Wetherbridge Square at noon on the fourth of July. *(He leans on the end of the bar and peers at Miriam's face. She doesn't look at him.)* The lady knows an unabridged in-cyclone of ways to be intimate with. Oh pleasurable yes—the prices are widely variable—I found them not inexpensive once—once—once— *(He laughs.)* I forgot we were entertaining. It was one of those diaphanous afternoons in August. You know that seem to drift skyward to some clearer space and then to another space even higher and clearer.

MIRIAM. You love August because you were born in August.

MARK. I don't think that would prejudice me in its favor on the first ballot. But you remember.

MIRIAM. It was memorable yes.

MARK. A crowded, lively party was in progress and I burst out of the star-chamber, my studio, bare-assed as when I first added my cry of protest to the. Shambled dizzily to the. Opened the sliding glass doors, noticed the presence of no one but my wife. Shouted to her, "God damn but I think I've done a painting!" I never did more than *think* I'd done one, you see.—Why am I so tired?—Nobody ever gave me a magnum or a quart or a baby's bottle of confidence, and I didn't have a long, white beard and a stepladder to the vault of the Sistine Chapel to paint the creation of creation.—Well, anyway, pretension is the unpardonable offense. *(His voice dies out: Wind chimes are heard.)* Put the words back in a box and nail down the lid. Fini.—Wait for me just ten minutes. Watch the clock and clock me. I'll remove the tissue and talcum my face and be back in ten minutes, exactly. *(He staggers, falls to the floor. Leonard crouches over him, quickly, and feels his pulse. Motions to the Bar-man.)*

LEONARD. Bar-man. *(They carry the body of Mark out of the bar. Miriam appears to see and feel nothing. The wind chimes are heard. The Bar-man returns, replacing the overturned stool to its place, crosses to* C. *table, takes the two glasses and returns to behind the bar. Leonard returns to the bar.)* Miriam, he's.

MIRIAM. I know.—A long ten minutes.

LEONARD. The concierge is making the. Arrangements.

MIRIAM. Released!

LEONARD. —Yes, he's released from.

MIRIAM. I meant that *I* am released.

LEONARD. If that's your feeling, it's one that shouldn't be spoken even to me.—How do you know I won't repeat what you said? We live in a gossipy world. I might accidentally, but.

MIRIAM. I'm sure that you will repeat but it doesn't concern me at all.

LEONARD. I think we should leave this room, and.

MIRIAM. I've never been to a mortuary and I'm not going to visit one now.

LEONARD. Let's get out of the bar and sit in the garden. The Barman hears and understands the savage things you're saying. *(She lights a cigarette.)* Miriam.

MIRIAM. Leonard. *(Wind chimes.)* —There's an edge, a limit to the circle of light. The circle is narrow. And protective. We have to stay inside. It's our existence and our protection. The protection of our existence. It's our home if we have one.

LEONARD. Not to be trusted always.

MIRIAM. You know and I know it's dangerous not to stay in it. There's no reason to take a voluntary step outside of the. Do you understand that? *(He nods.)* Miriam Conley is not going to step outside the circle of light. It's dangerous, I don't dare to or care to. This well-defined circle of light is our defense against. Outside of it there's dimness that increases to darkness: never my territory. It's never been at all attractive to me. When someone at a party says "Let's all go to the new club on something street, or even out of the country," I say "Wonderful. Let's go." With Mark? No! Mark was bored with this party before it started, But oh I go. Do I go! The circle of light stays with me. Until. Until can be held off but not forever eluded. You've seen how fatal it is to step out of the.

LEONARD. I'm not sure I know what you mean.

MIRIAM. Animation. Liveliness. People at a smart restaurant talking gaily together. Interested in jewelry, clothes, shopping, shows. Leonard, you know it's imperative for us to stay inside of. As for the others. You know and I know incurably ill people, especially those with dreaded diseases such as. And people gone mad that need an acre of pacifying meadows, trees around them. *(Tinkling chimes.)* A few perfunctory visits is all that they can expect and all they'll receive. Ask God if you don't believe me. It's like they'd violated a law that's.

LEONARD. Inviolable.

MIRIAM. Yes. Double yes. The circle of light won't be and can't be extended to include them. The final black needle is their visitor, Leonard.

LEONARD. Take this handkerchief and pretend to cry.

MIRIAM. I'll pretend to do nothing.

LEONARD. Let me tell you something that. When my grandmother died, after an agony of several hours, my mother called a correct undertaker, and then said to us "She put up a good fight. Now come downstairs and I will make us some cocoa and some cinnamon toast." We were children, but even so I thought the suggestion was shockingly inappropriate to the agony and death of her mother. Completed a minute before.

MIRIAM. She was in the circle that attends us faithfully as long as our bodies don't betray us and our minds don't make excursions of a nature that's incompatible with the.

LEONARD. Well.

MIRIAM. He was removed so quickly. If I should say that the circle of light is the approving look of God it would be romantic which I refuse to be. The program for today should not be changed except for the.

LEONARD. Absence of Mark.

MIRIAM. Mark that made the mistake of deliberately moving out of the.

LEONARD. Yes, Mark's absence.

MIRIAM. Of the man who has made a crossing that neither of us but each of us. I will bow my head to the table as an appearance of being stricken with. Then when we go to the street, put your arm about me as if I were overcome with the expected emotion.

LEONARD. Have you got everything, dear?

MIRIAM. It would be strange but possible if later I discovered that I cared for him deeply in spite of. He thought that he could create his own circle of light.

LEONARD. Miriam, what are your actual plans?

MIRIAM. I have no plans. I have nowhere to go. *(With abrupt violence, she wrenches the bracelets from her arms and flings them to her feet. The stage darkens.)*

End of Play

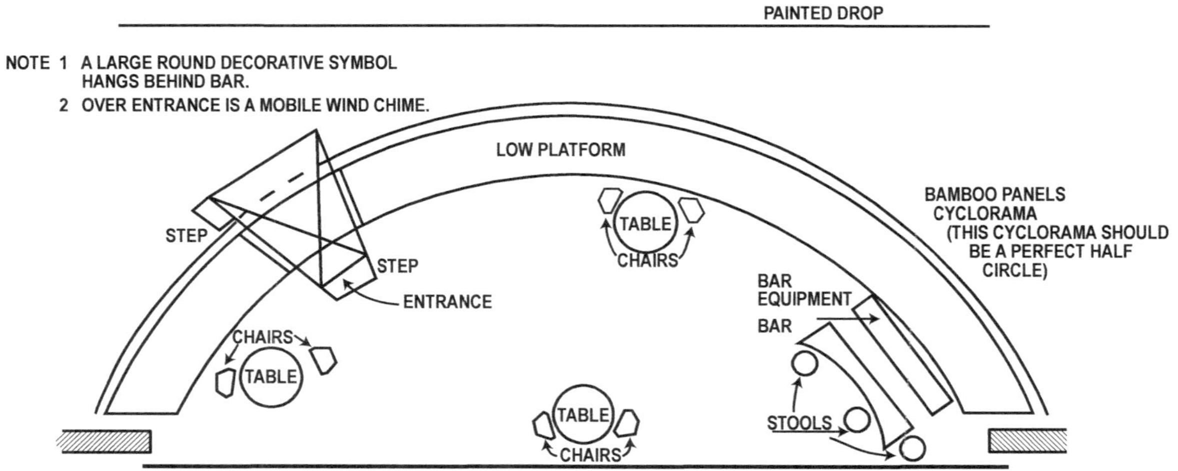

SCENE DESIGN

"IN THE BAR OF A TOKYO HOTEL"

PROPERTY LIST

(Use this space to create props lists for your production)

SOUND EFFECTS

(Use this space to create sound effects lists for your production)

Note on Songs/Recordings, Images, or Other Production Design Elements

Be advised that Dramatists Play Service, Inc., neither holds the rights to nor grants permission to use any songs, recordings, images, or other design elements mentioned in the play. It is the responsibility of the producing theater/organization to obtain permission of the copyright owner(s) for any such use. Additional royalty fees may apply for the right to use copyrighted materials.

For any songs/recordings, images, or other design elements mentioned in the play, works in the public domain may be substituted. It is the producing theater/organization's responsibility to ensure the substituted work is indeed in the public domain. Dramatists Play Service, Inc., cannot advise as to whether or not a song/arrangement/recording, image, or other design element is in the public domain.

NOTE ON BILLING

Anyone receiving permission to produce IN THE BAR OF A TOKYO HOTEL is required to give credit to the Author as sole and exclusive Author of the Play on the title page of all programs distributed in connection with performances of the Play and in all instances in which the title of the Play appears, including printed or digital materials for advertising, publicizing or otherwise exploiting the Play and/or a production thereof. Please see your production license for font size and typeface requirements.

Be advised that there may be additional credits required in all programs and promotional material. Such language will be listed under the "Additional Billing" section of production licenses. It is the licensee's responsibility to ensure any and all required billing is included in the requisite places, per the terms of the license.

IN THE BAR OF A TOKYO HOTEL is presented by arrangement with Dramatists Play Service, Inc. on behalf of The University of the South, Sewanee, Tennessee.

ALL TENNESSEE WILLIAMS PLAYS

The Play must be performed as published in the DPS authorized edition. It is understood that there will be no nudity in the Play unless specifically indicated in the script and that nothing in the stage presentation or stage business will alter the spirit of the Play as written.

www.ingramcontent.com/pod-product-compliance
Lightning Source LLC
Jackson TN
JSHW070543180826
106902JS00029B/996
* 9 7 8 0 8 2 2 2 0 5 6 2 3 *